The Valentine's Day Curse

Written by Frank Pedersen
Illustrated by Jeff Lai

Contents

Meet the Characters

Dr Anika Choudhry

A virology researcher.

Dr Alexei Morgenstern

Head of research.

Tony

A security guard.

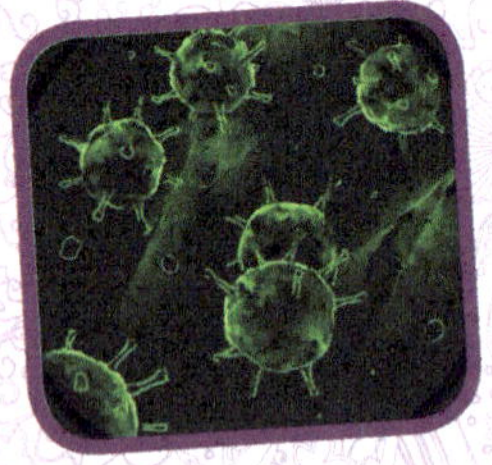

Congo-Heshangele

A deadly virus.

Dear Reader

Here's a Valentine's Day adventure with a twist. It starts out like all Valentine's Days, with a mysterious bouquet of roses. However, with mad scientists, deadly viruses and top-secret laboratories, it quickly turns into a gripping drama. This is one Valentine's Day you definitely don't want to share with anyone else!

Frank Pedersen

Author

The Underground Laboratory

1. Entrance
2. Security screening
3. Elevator
4. Level 4

1 Roses

When she answered the knock at her door and found the courier standing there, shivering in the gusty February winds, her first reaction was that he'd arrived at the wrong address. Bearing a bouquet of long-stemmed red roses that were neatly enclosed in cellophane wrapping, he winked at her and held out the flowers.

"Someone's got a secret admirer," smiled the courier. "Happy Valentine's Day."

Doctor Anika Choudhry was dumbfounded. "Are you certain?" she said.

The courier checked his delivery docket and nodded. "705 Brightwater Boulevard," he confirmed. "You're Anika Choudhry, right?"

Anika's astonishment was slowly overtaken by curiosity. She found herself nodding. "I am," she said.

“In that case, you definitely do have a secret admirer,” chuckled the courier. “Signature here, please.”

Anika signed the delivery docket and hurried back inside, cradling the bouquet of flowers. She realised she was smiling. After yesterday's drama, a romantic gift from a secret admirer on Valentine's Day was definitely the last thing she'd anticipated. But who on earth could the flowers possibly be from? She had only been in Mt Eleanor for a month, and she hardly knew anybody in this town. She looked at the copy of the delivery docket that the courier had handed her, but there was no hint of her mysterious admirer's identity.

"No sender's name, no address," she mused. "There's not even a florist's business card, so I can't work out what part of town they live in." She filled a vase with water and arranged the bouquet of roses neatly in the middle of her kitchen table. "Well, well," she said to herself. "Life is full of surprises."

Her thoughts were consumed by what she had to do today. She wasn't looking forward to it.

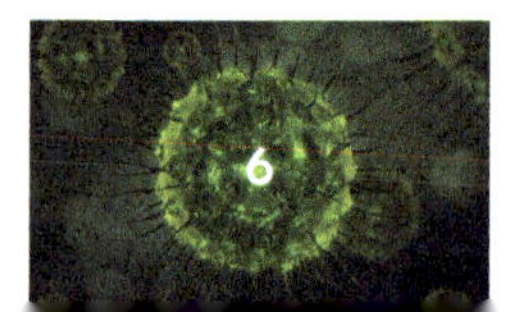

This strange surprise, at least, provided some momentary distraction from the uncomfortable feeling of foreboding rising in her stomach. The heady perfume of the roses filled her kitchen and she took a deep breath, filling her nostrils with the rich scent. Try as she might, she couldn't stop smiling. As a dedicated scientist, Anika spent her waking hours being rational and measured – but as a human being, she had to admit, she quite liked this other feeling, a mixture of mystery and delight. Someone, somewhere, had thought of her. She ignored the remainder of her uneaten breakfast and stared at the roses until she realised she was running late. It was critical she arrived first at the laboratory that morning. She took one last, deep breath, grabbed her car keys and headed for the door.

On the thirty-minute commute, she wondered who would have known her home address. She'd kept to herself since moving here, and anyone who asked her occupation had been fobbed off with a

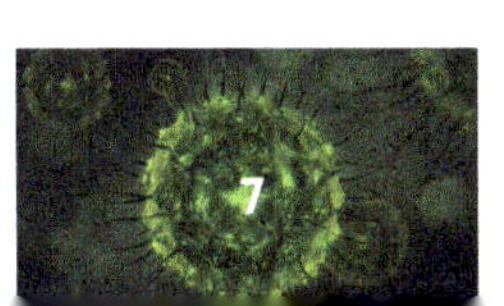

vague, non-committal answer. Telling the truth would make anyone feel awkward. As well as being a conversation-stopper, revealing her true work was also against the strict rules designed to maintain confidentiality.

Her boss knew her address, but she was convinced he had no romantic thoughts towards her, especially after yesterday's outburst. Who else at the laboratory knew her address? Then she smiled. There was someone she'd seen every morning and evening since starting, someone who always made an effort to be pleasant to her.

"Tony," she said to herself. "Did you look up my details on the security system? That was naughty. Naughty but nice."

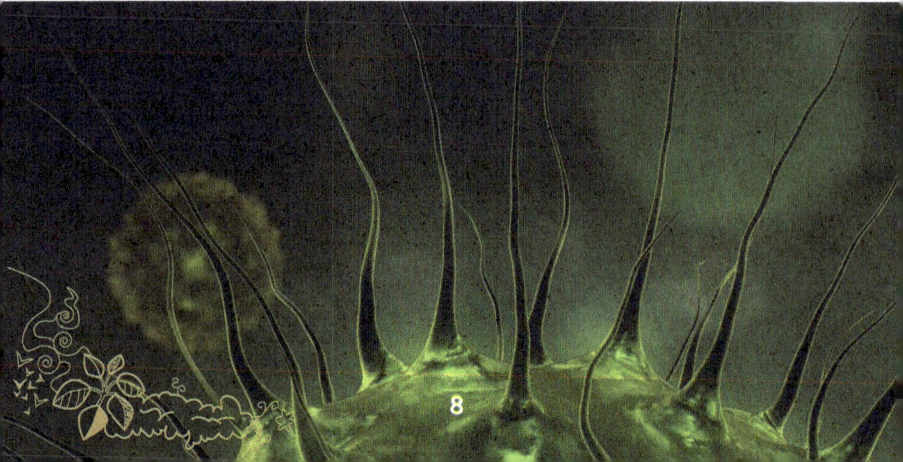

2 Congo-Heshangele

Three weeks earlier, Anika's day had started like any other. She was getting used to her new job and her new routine – a hurried piece of toast, a quick glance at the newspaper headlines, then a thirty-minute commute to the desolate, winding road leading to the granite outcrop that gave Mt Eleanor its name.

The security guard at the entrance to the laboratory grounds scrutinised her identification card, then waved at a second security guard behind the bullet-proof glass in the security booth. The gates in front of her slowly opened.

"Thank you, Doctor Choudhry," said the guard, as he returned the ID card. "Have a nice day."

Anika nodded and accelerated towards the parking area, finding a space next to a shiny black Cadillac SUV. It belonged to her boss: Doctor Alexei Morgenstern, chief virologist and head of the research division. Anika looked at her wristwatch and shook her head. It was only 7.00 am. Her new boss was strange and often seemed moody – but he was dedicated. The chief virologist was always the first in the laboratory, and last to leave.

"Morning, Tony," said Anika, as she walked into the entrance of the laboratory and handed her handbag to the security guard.

"Morning, Doctor Choudhry," replied the guard cheerfully. He took the handbag that Anika placed on the steel table and passed it through the X-ray machine. Anika walked through the body scanner and waited.

"Anything planned for the weekend? They're forecasting stormy weather," smiled Tony, peering at the X-ray screen. He picked up Anika's handbag. "Mind if I take a look?"

"Go ahead," replied Anika. She realised the X-ray would have picked up the small foil sheet of aspirin she'd popped in her handbag that morning. "Bit of a headache today," she explained, as the security guard examined the tablets.

"It's only Wednesday," said Tony wryly.

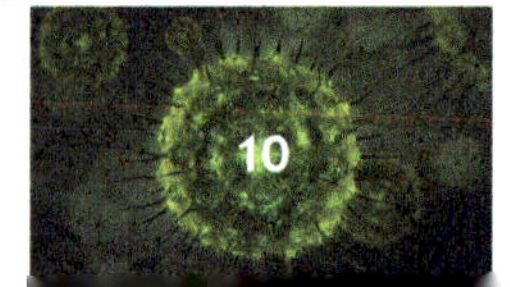

"Three whole days until the weekend. I'd be complaining of a headache, too, if I didn't love my job so much."

"Yeah, right," laughed Anika. Like most people in the high-security facility, Tony took his job seriously, but that didn't prevent him from having a sense of humour. Without it, working in a place where a slow, lingering death was only a mishap, a stumble or a clerical error away could prey on your mind. Maybe that's why Doctor Morgenstern seemed a little remote. He'd been at the laboratory for years, and he spent more time with viruses than humans.

"Good to go, Doctor Choudhry," said Tony, putting the aspirin back and handing Anika her handbag. "Have a lovely day, and pass on my regards to the friendly inmates."

"I certainly will, Tony," smiled Anika, heading for the elevators. "It'll make their day."

A palm print, an iris scan and a six-digit number combination. All three were needed before the elevator would descend to level four, buried securely within the rocky depths of the granite outcrop.

The elevator doors slid open and Anika walked towards the sterile containment area. She looked into another iris-scanning machine and waited while the computer matched the intricate details of her eyes with the database. A light flashed green and the automatic doors opened. Once she was inside, the doors closed behind her and, fifteen seconds later, when the powerful air filters had completed their task, another set of doors opened and Anika entered the laboratory. She slipped on her laboratory coat and headed for the coffee machine.

Someone with a morbid sense of humour had labelled the regular coffee pot "Vaccine" and the decaffeinated coffee "Placebo". Anika poured herself some full-strength vaccine, and headed towards her desk.

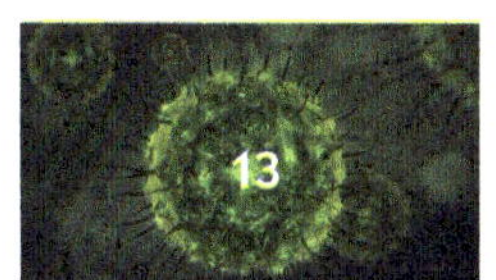

"Morning, Anika," came a voice from one of the glass-panelled offices lining the laboratory. "Ready for another day at the zoo?"

Anika nodded at Doctor Alexei Morgenstern. "You're here early," she observed.

"Our friends never sleep," he replied matter-of-factly. "Day or night, they're finding innovative, highly efficient ways to kill."

Doctor Anika Choudhry suppressed a shudder and walked to her work station. Time to begin.

The friendly inmates. Our little friends. These were the nicknames given to the deadliest mutations of the most virulent bacteria and viruses found on the planet, all of them held securely in the top-secret research facility known as the "zoo" by those who worked there.

Anika sipped her coffee and entered her password into her computer.

"C-H-I-M-E-R-A-1-3."

The chimera was a mythical, three-headed monster, a terrifying combination of lion,

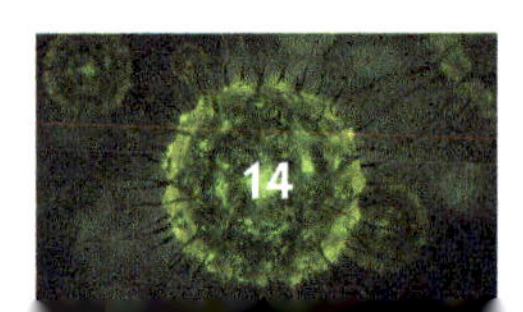

goat and serpent, which was highly aggressive, stubborn and deadly. The mutant virus she was studying, known as Congo-Heshangele-13, had all these characteristics and worse. At only 100 nanometres long, or a millionth of a millimetre, it was invisible unless you used an electron microscope. Nevertheless, it could irrevocably shut your body down within twenty-four hours.

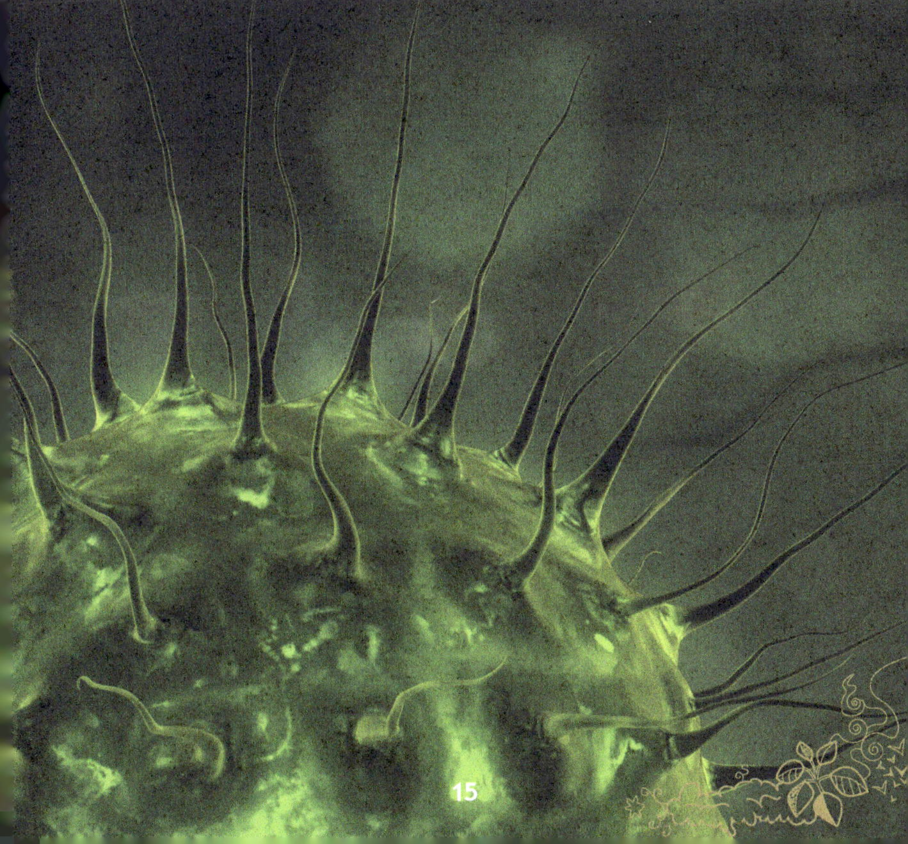

3 Bellerophon

If Tony, the security guard, knew that the future of the human race depended upon ten white mice, even his sense of humour would have deserted him. Deep within the zoo, Doctor Anika Choudhry had been monitoring infected laboratory mice, the culmination of a year's work by the gloomy Doctor Morgenstern.

At first, no one had worried about the severe illness that spread like wildfire amongst the chickens kept by villagers in a remote part of the Democratic Republic of the Congo in Africa. Then the pigs in the village started dying too. A microbiologist would have known that was a bad sign. A very bad sign.

An unknown virus jumping from species to species was dangerous, but an unknown virus jumping across different classes, such as birds to mammals, was extremely dangerous. It wasn't until the villagers of Heshangele started to

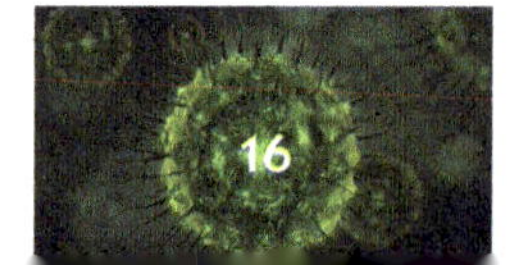

succumb to a terrible sickness that the medical authorities began to pay attention. By that stage, the virus was already in its third mutation. Luckily, one of the local doctors recognised the danger and alerted the authorities. By the time medical researchers arrived, Congo-Heshangele was in its fourth mutation, and people were starting to die. Not all the villagers had touched or eaten chicken or pork – so the researchers quickly realised that the virus was airborne, transmitted by simply breathing it in. Those who hadn't shown signs of being infected were quarantined immediately and treated with powerful antiviral drugs.

The outbreak had been contained – for now. But it was impossible to tell whether it had been stopped – or whether some variation of the virus was simply lurking somewhere, perhaps in the dusty soil, perhaps in the lungs of an unsuspecting carrier, waiting to reappear.

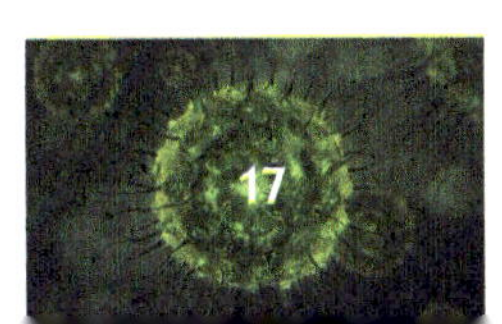

Doctor Morgenstern seemed strangely animated when he described how the sample of Congo-Heshangele-4 that had been brought back to Mt Eleanor mutated again and again, changing its genetic structure each five to six weeks. The instability of the virus actually brought him pleasure. Something so virulent, so changeable, had potential to eradicate the entire human population within months, he pronounced with a grim look of satisfaction.

"Isn't that amazing?" he asked.

"You've spent too much time isolated in this laboratory," thought Anika to herself.

A year ago, the antiviral drugs had worked – but within three months, the virus was so different that nothing available would combat the ever-changing strain. Through each of the nine mutations, Doctor Morgenstern had searched for some common thread, some element that each mutation shared. That, and that alone, offered hope for a pharmaceutical compound

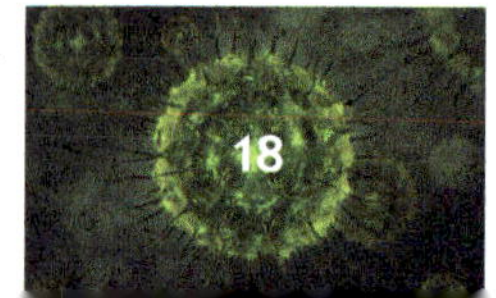

that might protect against whatever variation of Congo-Heshangele would appear next. If Congo-Heshangele-14 appeared – *when* it appeared – it would be ten times more dangerous. In the last few weeks, Doctor Morgenstern had isolated a promising pharmaceutical compound that seemed to be effective against the later strains of Congo-Heshangele. He'd grudgingly agreed for Anika to be transferred to the facility to help him monitor its performance.

Doctor Morgenstern used a long scientific name to describe his new pharmaceutical compound. But Anika had called it Bellerophon, after the ancient Greek warrior who'd finally killed the chimera. Before long, both Doctor Morgenstern and Anika were referring to the experimental drug as Bellerophon. If the drug was working, ten white mice would continue scurrying around their small cage, but if Bellerophon failed, the planet could face a plague the nature of which had never been experienced in human history.

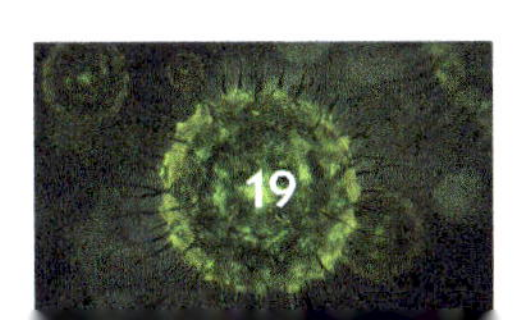

Anika's computer flicked to the remote-control cameras in the most secure section of the laboratory, Quarantine 3, or Q3. The room known as Q1 was reserved for naturally occurring pathogens: viruses such as smallpox and ebola, and bacteria such as anthrax and bubonic plague – deadly enough, but not as deadly as those held in Q2. Super strains, genetically modified pathogens developed by the military, and experimental vaccines to control mutations of other known viruses were held in Q2. But the inmates held in Q3 were special. When viruses were first discovered, they were described as "organisms at the edge of life". The vials in Q3 held the tiny fragments of genetic code that had the potential to push all life over the edge.

"How are my babies doing?"

Anika jumped with a start. She hadn't heard Doctor Morgenstern approach her work station. "Looks like all ten are still alive and kicking," she said, trying to regain her composure.

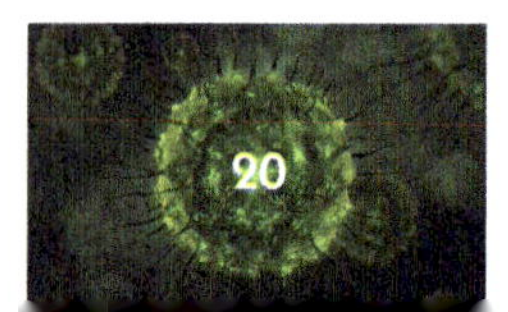

She pressed a key on her computer and the screen image zoomed to one of the mice. "No signs of distress."

"I meant the viruses," said Doctor Morgenstern coldly. "We should patent it," he added. "We'd make a fortune."

"Patent what?" asked Anika. What was her boss talking about?

"Bellerophon," he replied. He saw her expression, and forced a smile. "Just kidding," he said. After a week working with this strange scientist, Anika wasn't so sure.

"They're mammals, but they're not human," said Anika, referring to the mice. "The vaccine appears to work, but there's no telling how Congo-Heshangele-13 would react to it in a human body."

"Are you volunteering?" asked her boss, without a trace of a smile.

"No," replied Anika.

"Pity," replied Doctor Morgenstern.

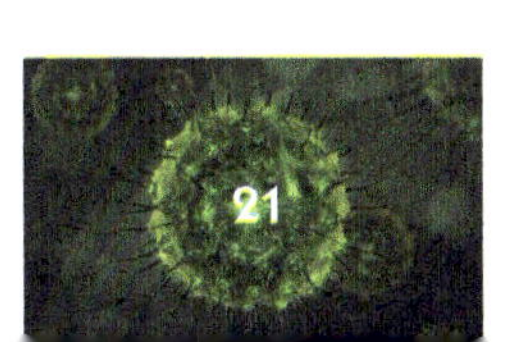

Q 2

"I've been waiting for Congo-Heshangele-14 to appear for over two months now," he continued. "But I suspect it needs live humans for its next transformation. One can only achieve so much within the confines of a sterile laboratory," he smiled wistfully. "If the mice are still alive by this afternoon, write up a report and move everything to Q2," said Doctor Morgenstern.

"Are you sure?" said Anika. "I think we still need dual access." No one could enter Q3 alone. Security dictated that at least two senior scientists were required at all times, to watch each other for the slightest error.

"Bellerophon has kept Congo-Heshangele-13 at bay for a week, therefore I consider it's reasonable to deduce we've found an experimental vaccine. Besides, I've got something even more exciting coming to the zoo: a nasty outbreak of something in an Amazonian village. Shaping up to be a real headache."

"Don't worry," replied Anika. "I've got enough aspirin for two."

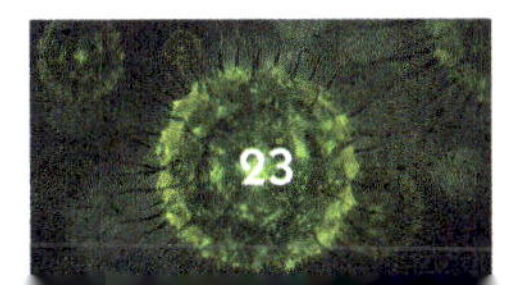

"No good to me," murmured Doctor Morgenstern, heading back to his office. "I'm allergic."

"All the subjects are still alive," reported Anika at two that afternoon.

"OK," said Doctor Morgenstern. "Let's get my babies moved."

The security protocol required two palm prints, two iris scans and two separate six-digit combinations. And that only gave access to the secure decontamination room. Dressed in full isolation suits, Anika and Doctor Morgenstern prepared to enter Q3.

An airtight door slid open and both scientists entered the most dangerous environment on Earth. For the first time since she'd arrived,

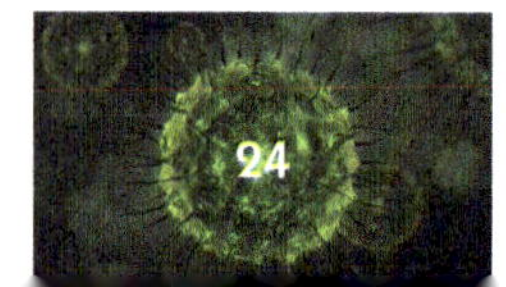

Anika noticed that Doctor Morgenstern was smiling. He was in his element.

They worked quickly, transferring the vials of Congo-Heshangele-13 and Bellerophon into a shock-proof container.

"And how are we this afternoon?" said Doctor Morgenstern. Anika thought he was addressing the mice, but when she turned around, she saw Doctor Morgenstern cradling a vial full of small white tablets: Congo-Heshangele-13. He saw the expression on Anika's face, and smiled once more.

"It takes ten trillion cells to make a human," he said. "And we're so arrogant, we think that we are Earth's dominant species. These guys don't even have cells. They're just fragments of DNA, a millionth of a millimetre long. Yet they have the power to kill anything. They're the real dominators. Humans are just gigantic, lumbering transport systems to these babies."

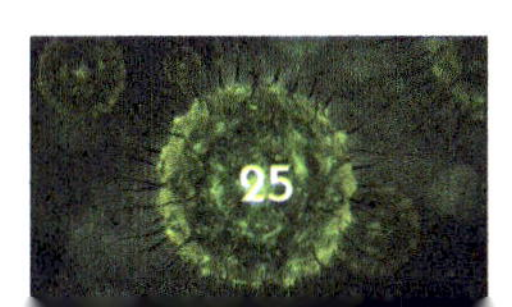

"Well, let's transport them and get out of here," replied Anika firmly. She was perfectly comfortable believing she was a member of the dominant species – but after a year working with Congo-Heshangele-13, Doctor Morgenstern clearly thought more of his viruses than of humans.

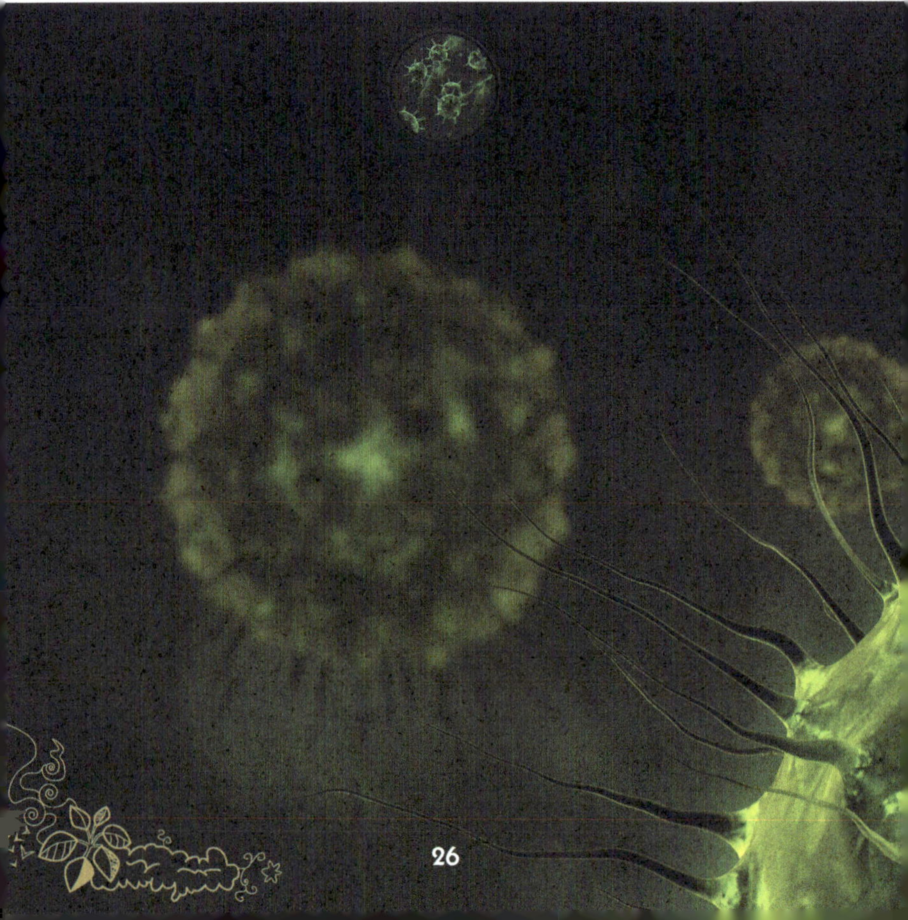

4 A Chilling Proposal

Two weeks later, Doctor Morgenstern was visibly disappointed. He looked up from the electron microscope. "Still Congo-Heshangele-13," he said dismally. "Something's stopping the virus developing into Congo-Heshangele-14."

"That's encouraging news, surely," ventured Anika. She was working with her boss in Q2.

"We're obstructing nature from taking its course," replied Doctor Morgenstern. "The most powerful force on the planet, prevented from fulfilling its potential."

"That's our job," said Anika.

"Our job is to observe and understand," replied Doctor Morgenstern, turning back to the microscope. "Interfering with nature is another thing altogether."

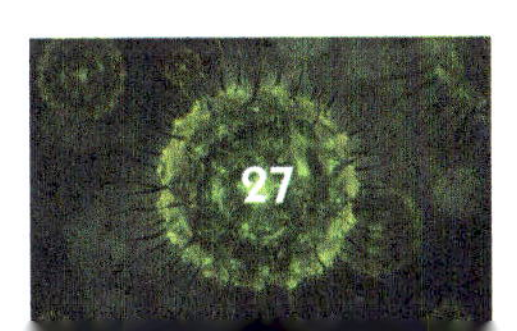

Doctor Morgenstern became more and more obsessed with finding Congo-Heshangele-14 as the days passed. The day before Valentine's Day, his obsession came to a head.

"You can't be serious?" gasped Anika, when she read the proposal Doctor Morgenstern had dropped on her desk.

"We have developed Bellerophon," he replied. "We can always deploy that before Congo-Heshangele-13 – or if we're lucky, Congo-Heshangele-14 – reaches its inevitable climax."

"But Bellerophon is completely untested in humans," protested Anika. "Even if anyone agreed to this madness, there's absolutely no guarantee that Bellerophon would work."

"When Doctor Jenner infected a child with cowpox back in 1796, there was no guarantee that would work against smallpox either," replied Morgenstern. """But it was successful, and it was the first-ever vaccination. Scientific knowledge progresses by taking risks."

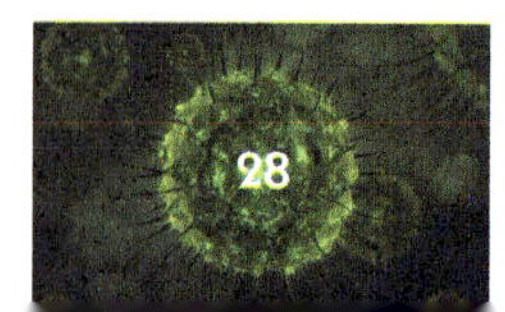

"But not these kinds of risks," said Anika.

"Without this, we might never observe the transformation to Congo-Heshangele-14," said Morgenstern.

"And that's exactly why we shouldn't do it," said Anika emphatically. "I won't agree to it," she said. "I will not be part of a human trial with a life-threatening virus. It's unthinkable."

With difficulty, Anika avoided Doctor Morgenstern for the remainder of the day. She couldn't believe that he would contemplate experimentally infecting a human being with Congo-Heshangele-13. If he mentioned his ludicrous proposal again, she'd have little alternative but to report him. Clearly, years working in an isolation laboratory had tipped him over the edge between scientific research and scientific recklessness. Morgenstern demonstrated more concern for his deadly viruses than he did for members of his own species.

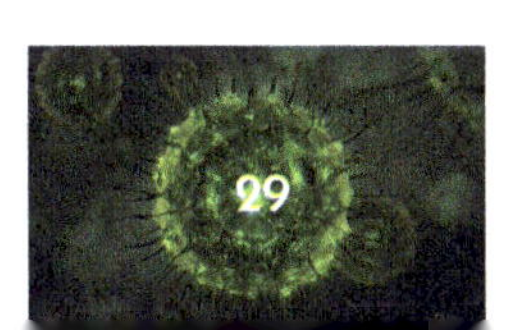

She glanced up from her desk and watched him working alone through Q2's double glass. "Mad," she muttered, returning to her research.

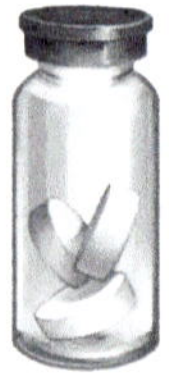

Half an hour before she was due to finish, Anika jumped with a start. Again, she hadn't heard Doctor Morgenstern approach her work station. She fervently wished he wouldn't continually do that. "Have you reconsidered my proposal?" he asked simply.

"No," replied Anika shortly. "And I won't reconsider. In fact, I'm going to report your proposal because, as a scientist, I consider you're in danger of crossing the line."

"As you wish," replied Doctor Morgenstern. He nodded towards Q2. "I've finished the procedures in Q2. The Bellerophon is located on the second refrigerator shelf, and is clearly labelled."

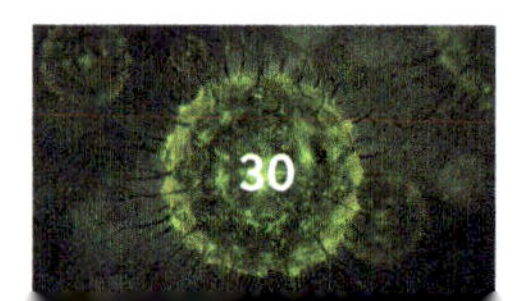

Q 2

"I know where the Bellerophon is located," replied Anika angrily. "I placed it there when we moved the experiment three weeks ago. And that's another thing that's been troubling me. In my professional opinion, Congo-Heshangele-13 is too dangerous for single access, and should be returned to Q3 immediately. I've a good mind to report that, too."

Doctor Morgenstern ignored her. "You know, blind testing is always the most satisfactory, because if a subject is unaware of the experiment, the results can't be clouded by personal interference. That's why we use placebos – harmless pills – as a comparison, because assuming the subject doesn't know which is which, the results aren't influenced by the subject's behaviour."

"So not only do you propose infecting someone with Congo-Heshangele-13, but you want to do it without their knowledge?" said Anika incredulously. "That's it. I've heard enough."

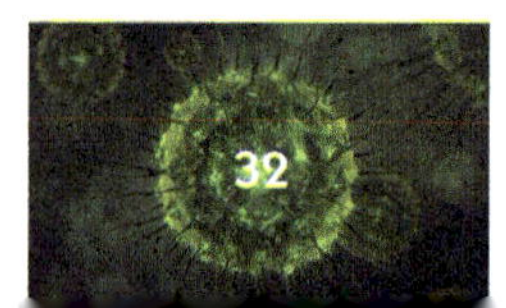

"Don't you want to the opportunity to observe the most powerful virus ever created?" asked Doctor Morgenstern. "Congo-Heshangele-14 could be the most amazing discovery this century, something so profoundly perfect in its microscopic structure that it could potentially eradicate the entire human race. And you could watch it evolve, right in front of your eyes."

"I don't want to see it," snapped Anika. "And, let there be no misunderstanding, I don't want to see you doing it either. I'm going straight to the senior management committee tomorrow morning, and I'll make sure this insanity is stopped immediately."

"You can't stop science," said Doctor Morgenstern with a chilling tone. "Expanding human horizons in the relentless quest for knowledge and understanding requires sacrifices."

Anika walked out of the laboratory. With a trembling palm print, a furious iris scan and

a violently entered six-digit combination, she caught the elevator to the ground floor.

"Everything all right?" asked Tony, the security guard, as Anika hurried through the scanner. Staff were rigorously checked when entering, and exiting, the laboratory. In this facility, nothing they brought in could potentially be as bad as what they might inadvertently carry out.

"It will be tomorrow," replied Anika evenly, trying to control her emotions. She'd made up her mind. She'd resolved to arrive early, before Doctor Morgenstern, and take her concerns to the highest authority.

"Didn't need these aspirins then?" said Tony with a smile. "You've been carrying them around for weeks."

"The headache I'm suffering from will need something a lot more substantial than a couple of aspirins," replied Anika. She grabbed her handbag from Tony, and headed for her car.

5 Valentine's Day

By the time Anika made it to the external security gates of the Mt Eleanor facility the next morning, snow was falling. She hoped it wouldn't turn into a Valentine's Day blizzard, like the weather event that had paralysed the entire north-east of the USA in 2007.

It was clearly freezing outside, and both guards were keeping warm in the security booth. Anika pressed her security pass onto her windscreen, fervently hoping she wouldn't have to wind her window down. Behind the bullet-proof glass, one of the guards peered at her windscreen and then, to Anika's relief, gave her the thumbs-up sign. The gates in front of her vehicle slowly opened.

"Thanks, guys," she said as she accelerated past, giving them a wave. She was thinking of the bouquet of red roses, practising what she'd say to Tony when she saw him. Then she'd call

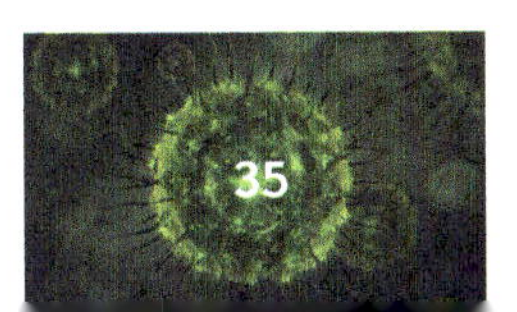

the facility's senior management committee and request an urgent disciplinary hearing, in a determined attempt to stop Doctor Morgenstern and his dangerous proposal.

Anika steered towards the vacant parking area. She was relieved to see that Doctor Morgenstern's shiny black Cadillac SUV was not yet there. Despite her pleasant start to Valentine's Day, she had an unpleasant task to complete. She looked at her wristwatch and shook her head. 6.45 am.

"How are you, Tony?" said Anika, as she walked into the entrance of the laboratory, trying to appear nonchalant. "Happy Valentine's Day."

"Morning, Doctor Choudhry," replied the guard cheerfully. Anika watched his eyes for any tell-tale flicker that would give him away, but noticed nothing untoward. "Happy Valentine's Day to you, too."

"He's doing well so far," thought Anika. "Who would have ever guessed?" Tony took the

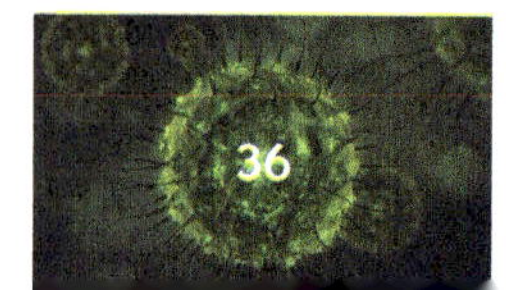

handbag that Anika had placed on the steel table and passed it through the X-ray machine. Anika walked through the body scanner and waited for her handbag. She decided to press Tony further.

"Anything planned for tonight? An evening with someone special?" she smiled.

"I'm not very romantic, Doctor Choudhry," Tony smiled back at her. "I'm not planning on spending any time with anyone."

"Really?" teased Anika. "Did you happen to send anyone any roses?"

Tony looked at her blankly. "You're kidding, right? Do you know how much florists charge for roses on Valentine's Day?"

Anika was nonplussed. "So you didn't have roses delivered to anyone, Tony?"

"I'm just a guard," he said, shaking his head. "I get paid to check people's bags, and even then, all I find is aspirin. Everybody's got a headache at the moment," he shrugged.

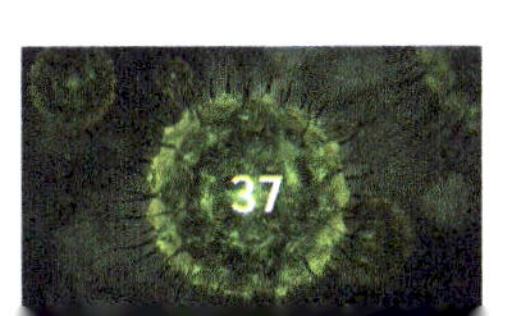

"Everybody?" said Anika, who was feeling half-embarrassed, half-perturbed.

"You, Doctor Morgenstern," replied Tony. "Everyone's carrying aspirin."

"Doctor Morgenstern?" said Anika in surprise. "He had aspirin?"

Tony nodded. "Sure," he said. "He had two in his satchel yesterday. And he's just called in sick, so they can't have worked. Something he ate, apparently."

But Doctor Morgenstern was allergic to aspirin. And then Anika's world started to spin. "No, no, no," she moaned softly. "You didn't."

She stood in the entrance to the laboratory, trying to calm down. But she couldn't. The facts ran through her head like lightning.

He'd insisted the Congo-Heshangele-13 was moved from Q3, a dual-access quarantine room, to Q2, where he could work alone. The Congo-Heshangele-13 was stored as white pills, easily mistaken for aspirin. He'd smuggled one out, along with a real aspirin to trick Tony. Blind testing.

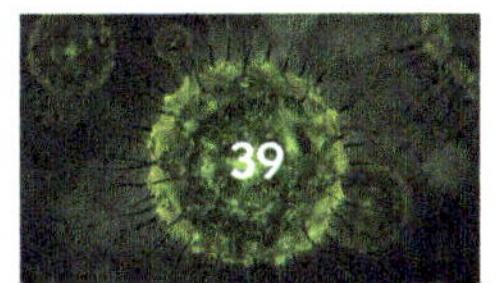

If Morgenstern had an aspirin and a tablet of Congo-Heshangele-13, deliberately mixed the two pills up, and took one, he'd still fall ill. It was the perfect double-blind test. Even he wouldn't know if it was just an allergic reaction or something worse.

"Wait," she whispered to herself. "It's not a double-blind test. Not unless there's someone else. There have to be two subjects. One with the real thing – and one with the placebo."

With a sudden chill, Anika recalled Morgenstern's last words. "You can't stop science," he'd said. "Expanding human horizons in the relentless quest for knowledge and understanding requires sacrifices."

Who was the second person being sacrificed? How could Morgenstern unknowingly infect someone with a virulent airborne virus? What seemingly innocuous delivery mechanism would he employ? What would make someone breathe in something, completely oblivious to its terrifying dangers?

6 A Curse Unleashed

The answer dawned on Anika with a rising feeling of dread. It was Valentine's Day. Her blood froze. The bouquet of roses. If Tony hadn't ordered them, there was only one other person who could have known where she lived.

Congo-Heshangele-13. Airborne. Tiny particles, ground into dust and sprinkled somewhere harmless. The perfect double-blind test. The perfect delivery mechanism.

She'd smelled the roses. She'd taken deep breaths. Not once, but twice.

Anika looked at Tony. An airborne virus meant anyone she'd been in contact with, shared a breath with, might be in mortal danger.

"What's the matter, Doctor Choudhry?" he asked. "You've suddenly gone pale."

"Tony, you're the only person I've been in the same room with this morning," said Anika. Suddenly she remembered the courier. But he'd

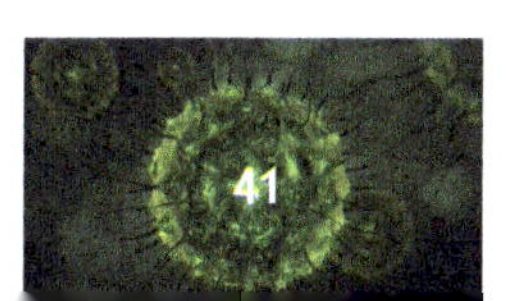

waited outside, in the gusty morning wind, and that meant there'd been little chance of a virus transfer. "We've been in this room, breathing the same air for five minutes."

"If you say so, Doctor Choudhry," said a bewildered Tony.

"Lock those security doors immediately," she ordered. "Do it now!"

Tony's usual smile was replaced by a look of fear. Doctor Choudhry was clearly alarmed. He hit the security button, locking down the facility.

"You're coming with me," said Anika urgently.

"Where?" said Tony.

"Q2," replied Anika. "There's about a gram of Bellerophon left. Hopefully, it'll be enough. Hopefully it'll actually work on humans."

"What's going on, Doctor Choudhry?" demanded the security guard.

"I don't have time to explain," replied Anika. "But what I do know is that your plans for today

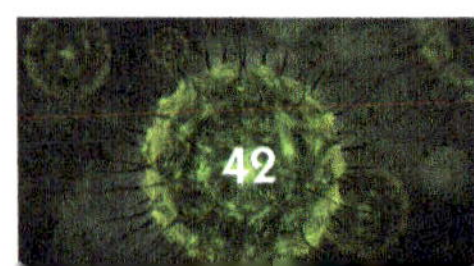

have suddenly changed, because you really are going to spend Valentine's Day with someone special."

Tony shook his head. He could tell something serious was going on, but what? "Someone special?" he said.

"Yes," replied Anika. "Someone so special they might just save your life," she added. "Follow me," she ordered.

Tony hurried into the elevator behind Doctor Choudhry. A palm print. An iris scan. A six-digit number combination. Anika hurried through the security procedure, conscious that every second, there was a fifty–fifty chance Congo-Heshangele-13 could be replicating inside their bodies.

A green light flashed, and the elevator started its descent to level four. Thoughts whirled in Anika's brain, and she desperately tried to remember the last heated conversation she'd had

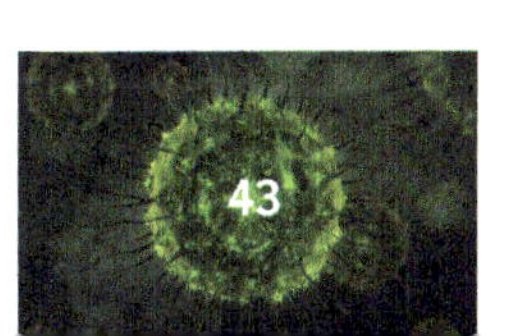

with Doctor Morgenstern. He'd talked about placebos. Had he crushed a tablet of harmless aspirin into a fine powder and sprinkled it within the rose petals – or had it been the real thing?

Right now, that was impossible to determine, but both she and Doctor Morgenstern, wherever he was, would discover the awful truth within twenty-four hours. Maybe he'd finally get to see his beloved Congo-Heshangele-14. Or, she thought with a shudder of horror, maybe she'd get to see it.

Anika led Tony into the secure environment of Q2 and double-checked that the doors were firmly locked behind them. "Happy Valentine's Day, Tony," said Anika grimly. "One way or another, this is going to be a date you'll remember for a long, long time."

She rushed to the refrigerator and, with relief, saw the Bellerophon right where it should have been. She was tempted to swallow it, right then and there, but she knew she couldn't. She'd have

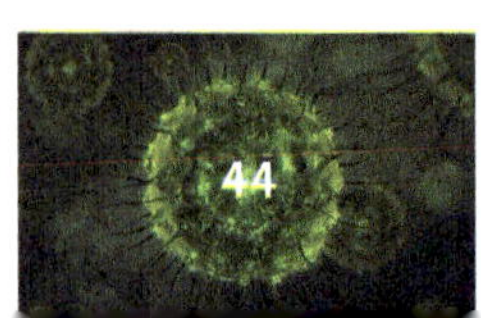

to wait. If the roses had been dusted with mere aspirin, Doctor Morgenstern, wherever he was, would need it. And if it were too late for him, anyone who discovered his infected body and breathed in the same air would need it.

She stared at the single dose of antiviral drug. If she'd been infected, at least she'd discover if it worked in humans. And if it didn't, at least she and Tony were isolated from the rest of humanity, deep within Q2. She picked up the laboratory phone and started to dial a long list of emergency numbers.

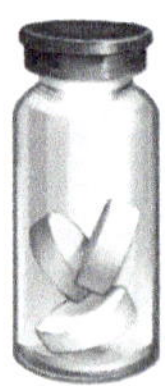

The Valentine's Day gales grew in intensity throughout the morning. Blizzards swept in and brought the whole town of Mt Eleanor to a standstill. It was the worst start to a Valentine's Day anyone in the area could remember.

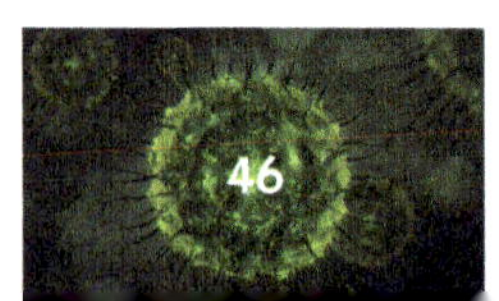

For one of them, it was about to get worse. Deep inside one of ten trillion human cells, a tiny fragment of DNA replicated itself imperfectly. Only a fraction of the original structure had mutated, but it was enough.

By the afternoon, one of two double-blind subjects would experience the truly terrifying fury of Congo-Heshangele-14. The Valentine's Day curse was about to be unleashed. The only question was where?

Doctor Morgenstern had made sure that his words would ring true. You can't stop science. As Anika waited, she just hoped that science could stop Congo-Heshangele-14.

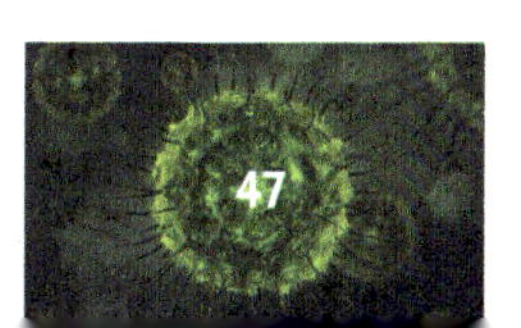

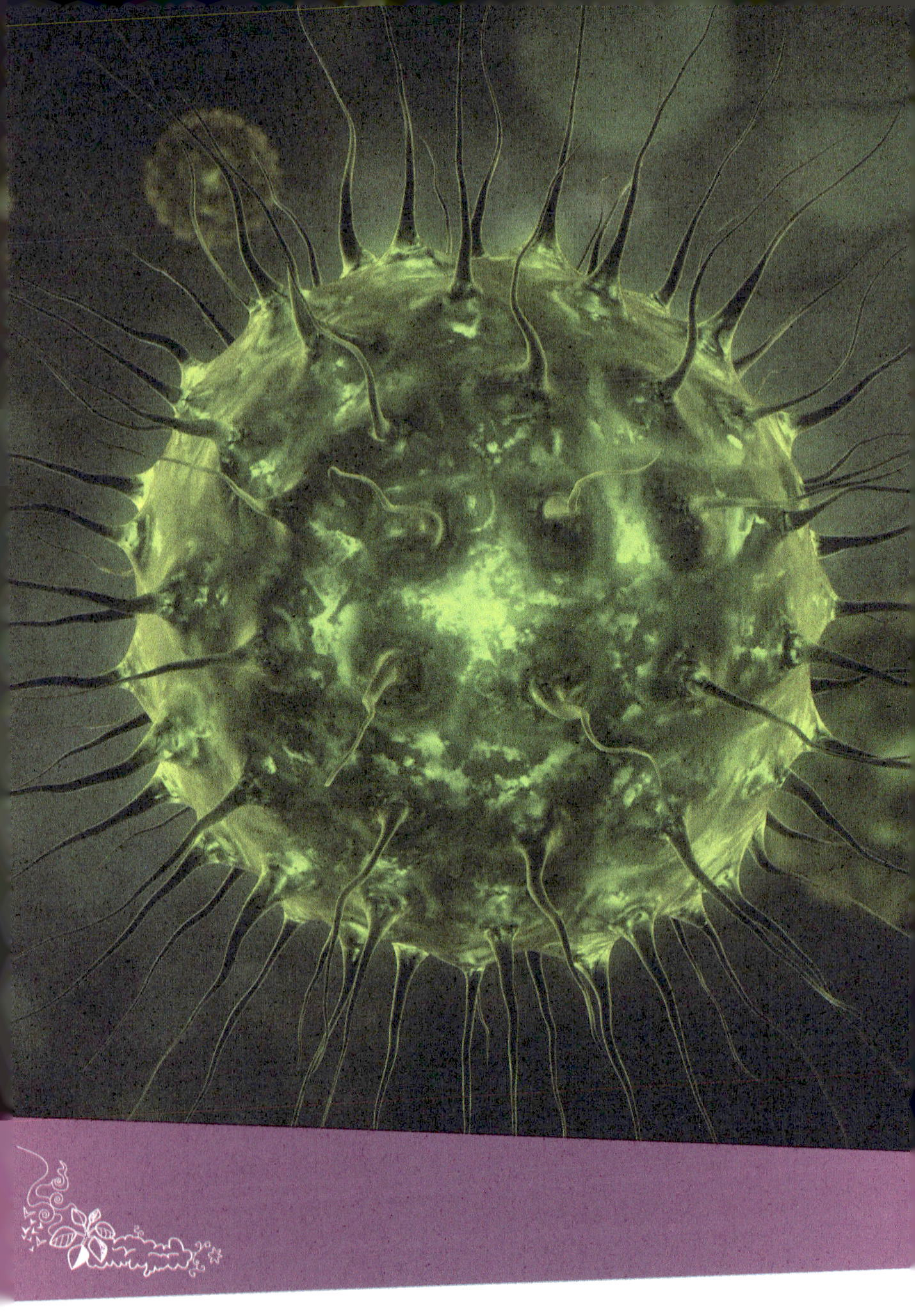